I AM EYES NI MACHO

I AM EYES

NI MACHO

WORDS BY LEILA WARD • PICTURES BY NONNY HOGROGIAN

SCHOLASTIC INC.

New York Toronto London Auckland Sydney

ISBN 0-590-40990-5

This edition published by Scholastic Inc.,
730 Broadway, New York, NY 10003,
by arrangement with Greenwillow Books, a division of
William Morrow & Company, Inc. BLUE RIBBON is a registered trademark of Scholastic Inc.

12   11   10   9   8   7   6   0   1   2/9

Printed in the U.S.A.

08

The sun wakes me.

I say,

"Ni macho!"

It means, "I am awake."

But it says,

"I am eyes!"

I see sunflowers and skies.

I see grasses and giraffes.

I see stars and starlings.

I see elands and elephants.

I see crabs and coral.

I see sun and sand.

I see the moon and moonflowers.

I see donkeys and monkeys.

I see coconuts and camels.

I see kites and Kilimanjaro.

I see flowers and flamingos.

I see pineapples and pelicans.

And everywhere

where I am eyes, I see butterflies.